JoJo & Gran Gran

This JoJo & Gran Gran storybook belongs to:

_____

First published in Great Britain in 2022 by Pat-a-Cake
Pat-a-Cake is a registered trademark of Hodder & Stoughton Limited
This book copyright © BBC 2022
JoJo & Gran Gran and the CBeebies logo are trademarks of the British Broadcasting Corporation and are used under licence
Based on original characters by Laura Henry-Allain MBE
Additional images © Shutterstock
ISBN 978 1 52638 373 0
1 3 5 7 9 10 8 6 4 2
Pat-a-Cake, an imprint of Hachette Children's Group,
Part of Hodder & Stoughton Limited
Carmelite House, 50 Victoria Embankment, London EC4Y 0DZ
An Hachette UK Company
EU address: 8 Castlecourt, Castleknock, Dublin 15, Ireland
www.hachette.co.uk · www.hachettechildrens.co.uk
Printed and bound in China
A CIP catalogue record for this book is available from the British Library

JoJo & GranGran

Go to the Hairdresser

Picture Glossary

Here are some words from JoJo and Gran Gran's trip to the hairdresser.

JoJo

Gran Gran

Charlene

Jared

Panda

shampoo

conditioner

comb

hair dryer

scissors

It was a summer day. The sky was blue and JoJo and Gran Gran were on their way to the hairdresser.

"I've never been to the hairdresser," said JoJo. "Mummy does my hair."

"Oh it's really fun, JoJo! I think you'll like it," said Gran Gran.

When they were nearly there, they bumped into Jared.

"Hey JoJo! Hey Gran Gran!" he said.

"Gran Gran is getting her hair cut today," said JoJo.

"So am I!" said Jared.

"But Jared, you don't have much hair now," giggled JoJo.

"I get my hair cut to keep it short," said Jared, "but my hair used to be much longer."

Jared showed them a photo of himself with longer hair.

 "WOW!" said JoJo.

JoJo and Gran Gran said goodbye to Jared and went into the hairdresser.

"Hey Gran Gran!" said one of the hairdressers. "I'll be with you in a minute."
"No rush, Charlene," said Gran Gran.

JoJo looked around. There was so much to see!

The hairdresser came over to JoJo and Gran Gran.

"Charlene, this is my granddaughter JoJo," said Gran Gran.

"And this is Panda!" said JoJo.

"We really like your hair, Charlene," said JoJo.

"Thank you!" said Charlene. "I like your hair, too."

"What are you having today then, Gran Gran?" asked Charlene.

"My usual trim, please," said Gran Gran. "Just a little off the ends."

Charlene took Gran Gran's hair down. "Shall we start with a wash?"

"Yes please!" said Gran Gran.

"Aren't you going to CUT Gran Gran's hair?" asked JoJo.

"Yes, but there are a few things we need to do first," said Charlene.

"You and Panda can be my special helpers, if you like."

"Oh, yes please!" said JoJo.

Gran Gran sat in the special chair by the sink to have her hair washed. JoJo held the shower head and directed the water onto Gran Gran's hair . . .

. . . and onto Panda!

"Oops!" said JoJo. "Sorry, Panda."

"Charlene always starts with shampoo," said Gran Gran. "So relaxing!" JoJo helped Charlene rub the shampoo into Gran Gran's hair.

"Now, we add deep conditioner," said Charlene. She combed it through Gran Gran's wet hair.

Next, Gran Gran went to sit underneath one of the big dryers.

Charlene gave her and JoJo a magazine to read.

"NOW is it time to cut Gran Gran's hair?" asked JoJo.

"Not just yet," said Charlene.

Charlene took Gran Gran over to the sink again to rinse out the deep conditioner. JoJo hadn't realised how much was involved in having a haircut!

Then, JoJo was given another job to do. Gran Gran moved to sit in the stylist's chair, and JoJo was given her very own spray bottle so she could help spray Gran Gran's hair.

"Is it time to cut Gran Gran's hair NOW?" asked JoJo.
"Not yet!" said Gran Gran.

Charlene combed Gran Gran's hair,

then dried it using a hair dryer that went

WHOOOSH!

"**NOW** it's time to cut Gran Gran's hair," said Charlene.

"Yay!" said JoJo.

"These scissors are very sharp, JoJo, so I'll do the cutting," said Charlene.

"Scissors are very sharp, Panda!" said JoJo.

Charlene snipped away at Gran Gran's hair, until . . .

"There we are! All finished," said Charlene. "You look amazing, Gran Gran!" said JoJo.

"Thank you! Charlene did a great job," said Gran Gran.
"Well," said Charlene, "I did have a fantastic helper."

"You're right, Gran Gran. Going to the hairdresser IS fun!" said JoJo.

Charlene smiled and said, "I do have some time before my next appointment if JoJo would like a little something too."

"Yes, please!" said JoJo. "Can I have it like that, Charlene?" she asked, pointing at a picture on the wall of a girl with twists in her hair. "Great choice!" said Charlene.

JoJo sat in a booster seat in the hairdresser's chair and wore a special gown to cover her clothes.

Then, Charlene separated JoJo's hair into sections using colourful hair ties. "Are you ready for the twists, JoJo?" she asked.

"Yes, please!" said JoJo.

JoJo looked in the mirror. "I love it so much!" she said.

"Thank you, Charlene."

"You're very welcome, JoJo."

"Wow, you look amazing," said Gran Gran.

When they got home, JoJo and Gran Gran sat on the sofa and admired their hair.

"I love going to the hairdresser!" said JoJo.

"Well, perhaps you could come with me next time, too," said Gran Gran.

"Thank you, Gran Gran!" said JoJo. "I love you."

"I love you too, JoJo," said Gran Gran.

Storytime Scramble

Here are some pictures from the story. Point to them in the order they happened and try to retell the story.